ISBN-10:1502835908
ISBN-13:9781502835901

DEDICATION:

To all my friends and especially the 1st Cumnock Boys Brigade, St Patrick's Primary School and St John's Parishioners. We hope you enjoy reading this First book in the Series and experience at second hand the delights and dangers of adventure in the Mysterious Castle.

CONTENTS

ACKNOWLEDGMENTS

I would like to say thank you to my brother Garry who did all my drawings and traced all the difficult stuff for me.

I would like to thank, three girls in my school, Molly, Holly and Sophie for giving me lots of inspiring ideas and so, I put them in my book for being really helpful. Morgan in my book is a really good friend of mine and him and his big brother stand at the bus stop with me and my brother Garry every morning.

I would like to thank my mum for typing all my scribbles even when she could not read them and was very tired when my little brother kept her up all night. She always made time to sit with us and inspired us.

I would like to thank you, the readers, for buying my book and helping me raise money for the Boys Brigade in Cumnock.

I would like to thank my dad, Garry Savage for paying for my book to be published and for banning my kindle at night and suggesting I find something else to occupy my time – I did dad !!

Finally, I would like to thank Mrs O'Shea for encouraging me to read and write about my adventures

FOREWARD

The story of John and his family whose day started off like any other and then they ended up having an Adventure not to be forgotten.

John and his two brothers and three sisters find themselves stranded in the woods and think they have found a safe place in an old abandoned castle but soon discover that it's not as safe as they think.

1 THE FAMILY

John and his family live in Cornwall not far from a large castle surrounded by woods and trees. John's mum and dad work very hard to look after John and his brothers and sisters. John's dad is a Police Man and his mum looks after the children at home.

John is 12 3/4 years old and has attended Sword Fighting Classes since he was just four. When John was four years old, he was sitting with his mum and she was watching an old movie. In the movie, there was no guns, just swords and John loved it so much that he said to his mum. "Mummy, one day, I am going to be sword man". His mum smiled at John and said "Good for you John". "That's a clever boy". Little did Mum know that John was deadly serious and that John's love of sword fighting would only grow?

John takes his training very serious and attends sword training every Tuesday a n d Thursday and takes part in local competitions. John is training to be a Teacher at the Sword Training Academy. John hopes one day to win the World Championship for Sword Fencing and his family think he is heading that way.

John has three sisters who are triplets. Molly, Holly and Sophie. The girls attend ballet every Tuesday night. The girls are eight and are very different in personality. Molly likes to be the daredevil, Sophie is quiet and shy and Holly is the protector of the three.

Molly often plays pranks on her sisters. One day, Molly put a bucket of water at the top of the door and didn't realise her dad was coming up the stairs before her sisters and splash! The bucket fell on top of Dad who was not happy at all. You often hear him shout "MMMollllyyyyyyy, what have you done this time"?

Sophie is very gentle and loves to sing. She is part of the school choir and often sings to her brothers and sisters and entertains the family when we get together.

Holly; well what can we say about Holly? Holly is 30 seconds older than Sophie and thinks she is the boss of everyone. Molly likes to remind her that she was born first by a whole minute so she is the boss – it's always fun and games in the Savage house.

Little brothers, Garry and Morgan are 11 and attend Karate on a Saturday morning at the local church hall. Garry and Morgan are always competing against each other. Garry thinks he is the best at everything. John always says he is just the best…..at being annoying.

The girls do everything together and mum is always saying stay together and look after each other……..

One thing all the children have in common is that they like to get into mischief and play pranks. Like the time when John was eight and decided that it would be fun to climb into the air vents and pretend to be a ghost. How was he to know that the air vent was just a bit of plastic and thump he landed right on mum and dad's bed….boy oh boy, was he in trouble? Mum and dad were covered in plaster from the ceiling and John was literally as white as a Ghost.

Then there was the time that Garry decided to put his twin brother Morgan into the tumble dryer. Mum was putting the washing away and heard screams. Running down the stairs, poor Morgan's legs were the only things she could see poking out of the tumble dryer as Garry hit his bottom off the door. Garry is most definitely the boss of the two and he knows it.

Let's not forget the girls. Oh they are no angels. There was the time, that mum was in the kitchen making dinner and dad came home and said to her, "Good day dear"? "Don't ask" said mum, "Go see for yourself". Up goes dad, opens the girl's room door and what does he find – **three girls** – oh no **three ghosts** as the girls had decided to do battle with a family sized tub of Talcum Powder. To this day, dad still recalls just seeing three sets of big eyes. It took mum months to get the talcum powder out the room.

So there you have, the Savage Family...... What will they do next?

2 THE WOODS

One Friday morning, Holly, Molly and Sophie decided to go out to play in the woods. Their mum had told them to stay at the edge of the wooded area and not go too far. They were to be back by lunchtime for something to eat.

Molly was a girl who liked adventure and said to her sisters. "Holly, Sophie – lets go into the woods, let's go for an adventure and see what we can find". The girls were frightened and excited but Molly just strolled on. Sophie tried to run home shouting "I am scared" but Holly grabbed her by the arm and said "No need to be scared, stay with me and I will keep you safe". And off the girls went into the woods.

The girls wandered around and were excited to see lots of little animals running around. They saw a squirrel climb a tree and heard an owl in the distance. Sophie, started to cry – "I don't like owls she said – they sound scary". Molly said "don't be silly there is no need to be worried. I have got a compass and torch in my backpack and I know the way home".

About half an hour later they suddenly realised that they were lost and didn't know how to find their way out of the woods. The girls sat on some tree stumps not knowing what to do.

Holly said "Let's set a fire to keep us warm – don't worry I have done this in the brownies and I know what to do". Molly said "Sophie, Mum will come and find us when we don't go home so why not sing us a song and keep our minds off the woods".
Sophie began to sing a beautiful song and the birds gathered round to listen.

Back at home, mum looked at the clock and saw it was almost 2 o'clock and she began to get very worried. John was sitting upstairs playing his X-box when his mum shouted his name. "John, I am worried, your sisters have not come back from their walk. Where can they be? What will we do"? "Mum" replied John "They'll be fine – you worry too much. I will find them. Don't you worry I will bring them back safely".

It was almost three o'clock by the time John got to the area that the girls had told mum they would be playing. He knew they had been there because he could see Molly's hair band that she had been wearing that morning, lying on the ground. He knew then that despite what mum had told them, that they had gone into the woods and he realised he needed some help, so he phoned Morgan and Garry......RING-RING!!...... "**Hello, Helllllooooo**......" "Morgan, Morgan is that you? It's John. I can't find the girls. Look don't tell mum that I can't find them but I need your help. I think they have gone into the woods.

John's voice quickened. Morgan, Tell mum that you and Garry are coming to help me please. "**Calm down John**", Morgan replied. "**We are coming**". John's voice grew more anxious "Meet me at the edge of the woods by the old swing park – but **quickly** it is getting dark already, we must hurry".

The boys grabbed their bikes and said to mum "We are just going to help John get the girls, see you soon mum"

The Boys jumped on their bikes and raced as fast as they could to the edge of the woods to meet John.

When they arrived John was frantic and pacing around. "Where have they gone? I have looked everywhere". Morgan said "look John, we will find them together". We need to think here..... Garry shouted, "Wait, I see three sets of footprints they must have gone this way".

Morgan and Garry padlocked their bikes to an old fence and then all three armed with flashlights, walked side by side into the deep woods

Meanwhile, in the woods, Sophie had fallen asleep, Holly was worried about getting home and Molly was looking around wondering which way to go. Molly said "shall we go this way, it's getting dark and I can use my torch". Sophie woke up and said "**NO, NO, NO**, we must stay here and stay together – someone will be looking for us.

3 SEARCHING FOR THE GIRLS

It was now well past four o'clock and the woods seemed really, really dark. The owls were tooting and the trees were rustling and animals were scratching on the ground.

John, Morgan and Garry continued to follow the footprints until they suddenly stopped. "**Oh no**" said Morgan. "**Oh dear**" said John. "**Oh help**" said Garry. The footprints were gone and the trail had ended... Where were the girls?

The boys were looking at each other in horror wondering what on earth they would tell mum. Garry said "The trail is gone, where on earth can they be". Morgan replied "perhaps they have been taken by aliens and are up in space". "Oh don't be stupid" Said Garry, "this is serious". "We need to find them and find them fast". "John, John, what will we do?"

The boys wandered around for another half an hour and suddenly John saw some smoke coming out of an area in the distance.

"Look boys, come on.... This could be them".

The boys raced towards the smoke and suddenly Morgan tripped over a fallen tree and cut his leg. It was bleeding quite badly and Morgan was in a great deal of pain. Quickly, Garry remembered that at the BB's they had been shown how to patch up a cut and he said "John, John, give me your scarf.... Quick, I know what to do".

John took off his scarf and handed it to Garry, he looked on as Garry cleaned Morgan's cut using only water from his water bottle and some leaves to clean away the dirt. Carefully, Garry wrapped the scarf around Morgan's leg and managed to stop the bleeding. Morgan tried to get to his feet but his leg hurt so much he started to tremble. "Its ok Morgan, take our arms, we will do this slowly together", the brothers said.

Realising that things were getting serious and the girls must be so scared, John clambered up and said, I will go ahead and try to find the girls. You follow on and I will try to find help. Morgan hobbled helplessly using Garry's arm as support. They both continued to follow the smoke.

"Do you think we will find them Garry"? "Yes, Morgan, don't worry, the girls aren't silly, and they will have found shelter somewhere. Anyway, they will know we are all looking for them, I bet they are looking for us right now….. Come on, I can see John just ahead, I think he sees something!"

4 I'M NOT STAYING HERE

Now nearly six o'clock and pitch black, the girls were cold, frightened and crying.

As they looked around, all they could see was darkness. Tiny eyes were peering from the trees and eerie noises could be heard in the distance. The girls were huddled together and Sophie was sobbing to her sisters that she wanted to be home, she wanted to be home with mum.

"**This is all your fault Molly**", Sophie cried. "Mum told us to stay safe but you just wouldn't listen…. You always do this, why, why wouldn't you just listen….."? Suddenly, Sophie started to push Molly to the ground and was on top of her, shouting, "**Why, Why**"…. We are going to die out here and it's all your fault".

"That's enough" Said Holly. "**Stop it, stop it both of you**. We can't fall out with each other, we need to stick together. We need to help each other, please girls, and please stop fighting". Holly stifled a tear and tried to be brave for her sisters.

Suddenly in the distance, the girls heard a piercing cry, it sounded like an animal being strangled and the girls started to scream. "Hhhhelllllllppppppppppp!!

Molly stood up and said "**I am not staying here.** We need to get help and we need to find a way out of these woods".

No, No said the others but Molly would not listen. "**Look**" she said, "look, in the distance, I can see lights, I think there is a house over there".

"Quick, let's go, it will be warm and we can phone mum and let her know where we are. C'mon girls, let's go. I told you we would be ok. I told you I knew what I was doing"

Excitedly, Sophie and Holly jumped up. "**Yes, yesssss**, great idea… Let's go Molly".

The girls set of towards the light and felt much happier thinking that they would be safe ……….. Or would they?

Meanwhile, back at home, Mum and Dad had now launched a huge search party. Not just for the girls, but now their boys were missing too….

5 THE CASTLE

About ten minutes behind them on foot, John shouted ""Morgan, Garry look there's a light lets follow it". As John and Morgan got closer and closer they could see shadows in the window. They realised that they had found the old abandoned castle. They looked at each other their faces white with fear. The castle had a story, a creepy story to tell.

They looked again at the windows and could just make out figures…. They looked like………….. Aaarggh…… Morgan screamed "Ghosts, John, Ghosts, it's the Ghost Castle. Run, Run, Run".

They were just about to run when suddenly, John said…. Stop, there's the girls. Quick, we must get them, we must save them. They don't know about the ghosts…….

"MOLLY, HOLLY, SOPHIE!!!" shouted John, Morgan and Garry in their loudest voices. The boys ran inside the front door and John grabbed Molly, Morgan grabbed Holly and Garry grabbed Sophie.

Just then John said, quiet everyone, I hear something. He listened and then slowly he looked round the corner and he saw an army of Skeleton Ghost's coming towards them. John pushed everyone back and they all started screaming….. Help, **Help**, **Help**.

The Skeleton Ghosts continued to march towards them **trum, trum, trum** they sang. The scary creepy sound sending shivers down everyone's spine. The girls were crying they wanted to go home.

Just then, John had an idea "Get the girls and lock them in the library" said John to Garry "Girl's don't open the door to anyone, do you hear me? If you hear a scream, a shout, no matter what, you stay here and you stay safe. Morgan and I will find a way out of this. We will find a way to save us".

Safely, locked in the library, the girls and Garry huddled together, the girls sobbing and praying that the boys would be ok. "I wish mummy was here" cried Sophie. "We do too", Molly and Holly soothed "but sshh we must be quiet. They mustn't know we are here". Garry, held the girls close promising to himself that he would keep them safe from the Skeleton Ghosts!!!!

6   DEFEAT OR DIE

"There's got to be a way to defeat these ghosts John. There's got to be ". "I know, Morgan, I am thinking – legend has it there is a book in the attic and it tells the story of the Skeleton Ghosts. We need to get there, we need to see if there is something in that book that can save us".

"**Trum, trum, trum,**" . . . . . . the sound grew closer, the skeleton ghosts were almost upon them.

John and Morgan got a rope and tied it from the banister to the door, this should slow them down if they try to come up the stairs. John and Morgan hurried up the stairs, **trum, trum, trum,** the sound got faster, the sound got louder. John could hear his heart beating out of his chest.

"**Quick Morgan, run**"......... Suddenly, they heard a thud and turning round they saw a headless skeleton, the head had come off as he tried to go up the stairs. The skeletons, used their swords and hacked through the rope, **trum, trum, trum,** the headless skeleton continued to follow them. John, quickly saw two swords on the wall and pulling them off, threw one towards Morgan. We must try to hold them back. John and Morgan, fought hard. They hacked at the soldiers and using the stealth of a marksmen, John cleanly took the heads of four. Just then, Morgan, said "Wait John, Run up the stairs"

As John ran up the stairs, Morgan pulled a huge wall cabinet down and blocked the stairs trapping just for the moment, the Skeleton Ghosts.

At last, they reached the attic. "Lock the door" John said. "Quick Morgan, Quick." Locking the door, Morgan said. "Look there's the book, John, what does it say, John, **John**".

"Quiet, Morgan, I am trying to read….. It says, legend has it that the Prince of the Castle was killed here long ago and his army of soldier's vowed vengeance on all who walked on his land. The legend says, that there was treasure and the treasure vanished when the Prince was killed. John opened the book at the last page and it read…..

"I have 88 keys but no locks …… Yee, who finds the key to the treasure will set the Prince free and the curse will be gone."

"What does it mean, John, What does it mean. …. What key, where is the key…is where is the….. John, John? The castle, it must mean the castle. There must be 88 doors in the castle!"

Frantically, John and Morgan climbed out of the attic window and down the outside of the castle. Banging on the library window, they shouted for the girls and Garry to let them in. Quick, Girls, Quick, Garry we need your help, we have found something.

Stumbling through the window, John said "we have found a clue, we need to work out the puzzle and free the Prince and the curse will be gone".

"What puzzle? What puzzle?" Shouted Garry. "Well" said Morgan "We found a book up in the attic ….. And a clue it read" **"I have 88 keys but no locks".**

7 THE TREASURE

For, thirty long minutes, they sat and tried to work out what the puzzle meant. They thought of everything. They tried to count the doors in the castle, they tried all the books in the library….. One by one, they put the books down, one by one realising they were no use. Still no one came, no one came to save them.

The sound started again, **Trum, Trum, Trum**…….. Sophie, sobbed, Holly cried, Garry screeched…. "The Skeleton Ghosts they are back"….

Suddenly, Molly stood up and fell back, hitting herself off something… "Are you ok asked John…..? What's wrong, Molly, talk to me, Molly what's wrong?"

Molly, stood their silently, looking at something…… looking at something in the library……… Suddenly Morgan realized what it was. Morgan, cried out…. "Look John…. Look……Look at what she is staring at….. "

Everyone turned to look at Molly and realized she was looking at the Piano. "T h e Piano" shouted John, "That's it, The Piano." Repeating the puzzle he said…..

"I have 88 keys but no locks …… Yee, who finds the key to the treasure will set the Prince free and the curse will be gone."

The Piano, of course, the Piano has 88 keys…

The six children huddled round the piano, as the Skeleton Ghosts got closer, **Trum, Trum, and Trum.** By now they were banging on the door……

Garry said, "**Stop, Stop** John, I will hold them off. I will cause a diversion. Scrambling out of the window and climbing up the tree, Garry jumped back through the window on the first floor".

The sound of the Skeleton Ghosts began to fade and they realized that they had turned their attention to Garry.

Suddenly, Garry cried out... "**Help John I am trapped, Help, they have me cornered. Help me, Help me, Help.........**"

John ran out the study door to help Garry and shouted to Morgan and the girls, find the treasure, find the puzzle, and help me to save the Prince and Garry.

As Morgan and the girls frantically searched the piano, above them was the sound of clatter, the sound of breaking glass and the sounds of a terrible fight between the Skeletons and the Brothers.

In the study, Molly stopped dead in her tracks. Realising that the Piano held the clues, she played the music sheet that was on the Piano rest. Suddenly, a button appeared and together they all pressed it.

As if by magic, the Piano opened up in the middle and suddenly a bright glow appeared as the protector of the treasure came in to view. A loud booming voice said

"You have found the treasure but you must solve one last puzzle to free the prince".

You're almost at the very end, but where you will release the Prince is where you once came in, you must retract to find the Prince, you must go back from whence you came and never to return again.......At the point of no return, you will find a key, the key to unlock the curse, and set the Prince Free. You must put the key in the lock and turn It ONE, TWO, THREE then knock FOUR times and say HELLO, Prince of the Castle be free.

All at once, they all shouted, **"THE DOOR, THE DOOR, THE DOOR**, we must go out the door….."

Meanwhile, up the stairs, Garry was now cornered in the Attic. John came charging in the door and using his sword, took the head off the skeleton standing over Garry.

They heard the others shouting, quick quick, we must all go out, we must go out together….

Using all their might, they boys rushed the Skeletons and pushing them to the ground they jumped down the stairs to meet the others.

Just then, they turned round….. **Trump, trump, trump**…. The skeletons were hot on their heels.

Quick, quick everyone, we must go and we must do this together.

The six, ran out the door and as quick as a flash, Molly found the key hidden under a fallen oak tree. Squeezing her hand through the gap, she picked it up and raced back to the door.

We must hold hands, we must do this together. By now the skeletons were at the bottom of the stairs, Sophie, **Screamed.** We are not going to make it. Do it now Molly, **Do it now…….**

Molly, put the key in the lock and turned the lock **ONE, TWO, THREE**. They all knocked on the door together **FOUR** times and said **HELLO**, Prince of the Castle be free.

Almost at once everything froze around the castle except the six... One by one, the Skeletons crumbled to ashes on the ground. The castle suddenly lit up like a Christmas tree and as quick as it lit, it started to fade and sink into the ground like it was in Quicksand.

John shouted, "**RUN,** get out of here...... It will suck us under too... I will be right behind you".

Taking the girls, Garry and Morgan raced out of the Castle Grounds straight into a stream of lights.

Molly started to scream "**What about John, we can't leave him**". Garry grabbed her. "He will be ok, I know him like the back of my hand, and he gets out of everything".

Minutes later, the stream of lights became a stream of people and they realized this was the search party that their mum and dad must have sent out. The girls screamed and ran into mums arms. "We were so frightened mum, the castle, it was so scary, and the Skeleton Ghosts, mum we nearly died".

Mum and Dad looked around, "What castle, What Skeleton Ghosts..... .What are you talking about Girls and where is John?"

In the distance, they heard a voice. "I am here, Mum, Dad I am here. I am safe....." John appeared and they all hugged and mum and dad were just thankful they were safe and sound.

8 HOME AT LAST

Back home, they told mum and dad all about the Castle and all about the Skeleton Ghosts.   Mum and Dad looked at each other and then looked at the children

"The Castle children…. The one beside the old fallen oak tree?" "Yes Dad that one" said John……. "Kids, that castle was demolished 50 years ago. There is no castle, its only ruins……"

The children all looked at each other in horror. What had just happened to them today…. What had gone on?

They all went up to Johns room and talked about what they had experienced that day…..

"Did we imagine it all said Morgan…We couldn't have. My cut, look at my cut". Carefully, Garry removed the scarf and nothing was there. There was no cut!!!

"Was it not real?" said Garry…… "What's happening to us …?" Said the girls.

Their couldn't have been a castle, or a Prince could there?

Just at that, John pulled something out from under the bed. Carefully placing the box on the bed, he opened it and there inside was the Prince's Treasure, a key and a Map….. There was note with the map and it read.

"The Prince's treasure that ye found, was just a little offer, the pirate ship has bucket loads more to fill your coffer. So find ye ship and find the island, and find thee treasure trove, I give you this map and I give you this key, so start at the Orange Grove…….."

The End.......................................

ABOUT THE AUTHOR

John was born at Irvine Central on the 9th December 2004 and lives in Cumnock with his twin Brother Garry. He lives at home with his Mum, Roseanne and Dad, Garry Snr and his little sister Tyla and little brother Lewis. They also have a dog called Barmy Bess. John loves to read and write stories and this is the first in a series of books that John plans to write.

John would like to say a huge big thank you to his Granny Kate and Granny Jean for always been there for him as he grows up.

Printed in Great Britain
by Amazon.co.uk, Ltd.,
Marston Gate.